Helen Orme

Ransom

Odd One Out

by Helen Orme
Illustrated by Cathy Brett
Cover by Anna Torborg

Published by Ransom Publishing Ltd.
Rose Cottage, Howe Hill, Watlington, Oxon. OX49 5HB
www.ransom.co.uk

ISBN   978 184167 597 8

First published in 2007

Meet the Sisters ...

Siti and her friends are really close. So close she calls them her Sisters. They've been mates for ever, and most of the time they are closer than her real family.

Siti is the leader – the one who always knows what to do – but Kelly, Lu, Donna and Rachel have their own lives to lead as well.

Still, there's no one you can talk to, no one you can rely on, like your best mates. Right?

1

Birthday plans

Donna was walking to school with Siti.

"What are you doing for your birthday?" Siti asked.

"Dunno yet," said Donna. "Trouble is, it's on a school day."

"Yeah! It's two weeks on Thursday isn't it? We could do something the following Saturday."

"I'll have to see what my mum's doing."

"Yeah – cool. I'll talk to the Sisters and we'll start thinking."

The Sisters were Donna and Siti's friends. They were really close and did everything together.

Later, at school, Siti found the other three.

"We've got to get something sorted," she told them.

"We could take her to that new pizza place," said Rachel.

"What about swimming?" suggested Siti. "She likes swimming and we could eat afterwards."

That night Donna asked her mum if they were planning anything.

"We're going to be a bit busy that weekend," she said. "You can have your friends round to tea after school on your birthday though."

Donna thought that was a bit childish. "But," she thought, "at least I know I can do something with the Sisters."

2

Kid's stuff

Donna told her sisters about the tea party. Marie looked at Briony, and pulled a face.

"Sorry Donna, kids' stuff, don't you think Bri?" said Marie.

"I won't be here on Thursday anyway," said Briony. "I've got to stay at college – Drama Club."

"I'll be here," said Michael. "I like tea parties." Michael was Donna's younger brother.

"Yeah, well! Like I said, kids' stuff." Marie shrugged and went out of the room.

Donna was disappointed. O.K. – it was kids' stuff, but they didn't have to go on about it.

Donna's mum saw how upset she was.

"I'm sorry, love," she said. "It's just that things are a bit difficult at the moment."

Donna knew what that meant. It meant that they hadn't got much spare money.

Not much chance of a big present.

"I'll make it up to you later."

"Sorry Donna," said Briony. "I would come, but Drama Club is really important."

"It's cool," said Donna. "Anyway, I've got something planned with the Sisters for the weekend. You don't need to worry about me."

3

Something Special

Siti was cross when Donna told her about Marie and Briony.

"I know they think we're just kids, now Marie's working and Briony's at college," she told Lu later. "But it's not like them to be so mean!"

"We'll have to do something really special," said Kelly.

"I think Siti's idea's great," agreed Rachel. "Swimming, then a pizza."

"And we'll get her a really decent present."

Siti said they should keep it a surprise so they didn't tell Donna what they'd got planned.

All week the Sisters did their best to make Donna feel good. But it wasn't so good at home. Donna had tried to be happy about her birthday. The Sisters were great – but it just wasn't the same when her family didn't seem bothered.

Mum had tried to be nice and kept saying they'd do something 'later on'.

But Marie and Briony were still upsetting her.

4

Why were they being so mean?

Donna loved the Sisters, but she loved her real sisters too. They had always got on really well. They'd done loads of stuff together. Now neither of them seemed interested in Donna's birthday. Every time Donna tried to talk about it they changed the subject. Briony kept on about her drama club until Donna wanted to scream.

She tried to talk to her dad.

"Don't worry about it," he said. "Marie's growing up, that's all; and Briony wants to be grown up too. You stay my little girl a bit longer."

That was not what Donna wanted to hear. She didn't want to stay anyone's 'little girl'.

Worst of all Marie and Briony seemed to be cutting her out of everything. They were always hiding away in Marie's bedroom talking.

As soon as Donna walked in they changed the subject, or Briony got up to go out, or Marie plugged in her MP3.

It wasn't fair. Why were they being so mean?

5

Feeling shut out

Donna made a special effort to be nice to Marie and Briony. She did her best to be quiet and helpful when Briony was doing her college work. They shared a bedroom and Bri was always moaning that Donna made too much noise.

The worst thing was that Marie and Briony seemed to be spending all their time together.

She felt really shut out!

It was only three days to her birthday and she was sick of her whole family. Siti found her in tears.

"I don't know what I've done wrong!" sobbed Donna. "Why don't they like me any more?"

Siti tried to calm her down.

"It can't be you – you haven't done anything."

"Well, why are they being like this?"

"I don't know," said Siti.

"But I'm going to find out!" she thought to herself.

Later she found Kelly.

"We've got to do something for Donna," she said. "I'm going to talk to Briony and you've got to help me."

6

What have I done?

It was Donna's birthday! Things were just the same at home.

Worse still, now the Sisters were acting strange!

They were still promising to make Saturday special, but Donna noticed that they stopped talking and changed the subject when she got anywhere near them.

"They've all gone off me too," she thought. "What have I done?"

She decided the Sisters must be fed up with her moaning and moping all the time.

"Maybe they don't want to hang around with me any more," she thought.

They all seemed happy at the end of school as they set off to Donna's house. Michael had been sent off to his friends so it was just the Sisters.

"You can open your presents before tea," said her mum. Donna looked at the small pile of gifts and cards.

"Here are our cards," said Siti. "But you'll get our present on Saturday."

Donna began to open her presents. She got clothes from Briony and Marie, chocolates from Michael and some money from her grandparents. There was nothing from mum and dad except her card.

"I'll get your present at the weekend," said mum. "I just didn't have time this week."

7

Happy Birthday!

The tea party had been just as awful as Donna thought. O.K., Mum had tried her best to make it look pretty, but JELLY!

Who in their right mind would give jelly and ice cream to a fourteen year-old?

The Sisters had been great, though. They pretended that they were having fun, but Donna knew they weren't really.

Finally it was Saturday. The Sisters were taking her swimming. She was really looking forward to it.

"What are we going to do afterwards?" she asked.

"Well, it depends what time we finish," said Siti.

"We could go for a drink in the café," said Rachel.

"If there's time," agreed Siti.

Swimming was great and Donna felt almost happy. But when they were having their drinks afterwards it all seemed to go wrong again.

No one said anything about her present. They'd promised her something nice, but now it seemed as if there was no present at all.

Siti kept looking at her watch.

"She doesn't want to be here," thought Donna. She felt like crying again.

Siti jumped up. "Come on then, let's get going!"

Lu looked at Donna. She grinned. "Come on – you're going to love this!"

The Sisters pushed Donna gently towards the exit. Outside was a bright red people carrier with a banner saying 'Happy Birthday Donna.'

It was Lu's dad. He got out, opened the door and bowed.

"Your taxi madam," he said to Donna, as he opened the car door for her. She got in the front and the others squashed into the back.

Soon they were at Donna's house. There was another birthday banner over the front door and barbecue smoke coming from the back garden. Marie opened the gate and Donna saw that the garden was full of people.

"Happy Birthday!" they all yelled.

"Welcome to your birthday barbie!" said Marie, giving Donna a big hug.

Then Donna did something really stupid – she burst into tears.

"I'm so happy," she sobbed. "I thought no one cared."

Her mum came over. "Of course we care," she said. "Marie and Briony wanted to do something really special for you."

Donna looked at Siti. "You all knew too, didn't you?"

"Only a few days ago," said Siti.

"We talked to Briony," said Kelly. "She explained it all."

"Present time," said Briony and pulled Donna over to a table. "Look what mum and dad got you. It's what you've always wanted."

"And here's ours," said Siti, picking a box from the table and handing it to Donna.

Donna looked at the presents, then at her friends, then at her sisters. Michael came over and gave her a big hug. She hugged him back.

"I've got all you lot," she said. "That's all I ever wanted."